Taken by The Mountain Man

Kaci Rose

Five Little Roses Publishing

Copyright

Publisher's Note: This is a work of fiction. Names,

characters, places, and incidents are a product of the author's imagination.

Locales and public names are sometimes

Book Cover By: **Cormar Covers**
Editing By: **Violet Rae**

Blurb

He's a scarred up mountain man. She is the curvy girl no one wants until him. Who knew she'd be the one to save him. And I sure

Cole

Go in and save my friends girl. That was the mission. I never expected her, the girl who wasn't supposed to be there.

She's injured... and mine.

So, I take her back to my cabin to care for her.

Only she wasn't supposed to want to leave...

I have no problem holding her against her will until that first tear falls...

Jana

I never expected to be kidnapped by my best friend's mother and I also never expected to be rescued by a strange sexy mountain man.

Yes, this is currently my life.

When this strong and slightly scary man takes me back to his cabin, I have no idea what to expect.

But it wasn't how gentle he is and how much he takes care of me.

And I sure as hell wasn't expecting to fall in love with him.

Too bad I can't stay.

Dedication

To all who think of running off to the mountain and leaving everyday life behind, even just for a weekend.

Contents

Get Free Books!

Do you like Military Men? Best friends brothers?
What about sweet, sexy, and addicting books?

If you join Kaci Rose's Newsletter you get these books free!

https://www.kacirose.com/free-books/
Now on to the story!

Chapter 1

Jana

F uck, why does my head hurt so much?

As I open my eyes, I realize it's because the kidnapping wasn't a nightmare. It's real—a *living* nightmare. I've been in this cabin for what seems like forever. They've drugged me here and there, but I think it's been two or three days.

I returned from visiting my best friend, Hope, and her boyfriend, Cash, who lives on the mountain. I live in an apartment above the cafe in the grocery store where I'm the general manager. The parking lot is behind the building, and I was pulling my keys out of my purse when I was grabbed from behind. I remember the pinprick on my arm before everything went black, and I woke up in this cabin.

Of all the sick and twisted things, the people who kidnapped me are Hope's mom and her boyfriend. They've been trying for days to get information out of me and to get me to call Hope and have her meet me somewhere so they can kidnap her, which I refused to do.

The first time I refused, the boyfriend took a baseball bat to my ankle. To say it hurt like hell would be an understatement. Since then, I've been starved and hit in the head, and they've stomped on my injured foot several times. The last time I refused to speak, they burned my arm with one of their cigarettes.

A quick look around the cabin reveals I'm alone, which means they're outside or in the other room going at it like rabbits, which is what they seem to like to do in their free time. So once again, I try to work on freeing my hands strapped behind me.

I only get a few minutes before Hope's mom walks in, and the boyfriend is right behind her. They're high on something, though I have no idea what. I can see it in their eyes and behavior because they never sleep.

Her mom walks over and shoves a piece of bread in my mouth. I try to chew as fast as possible because they've taken it away if I take too long. Once I finally swallow it, they tip my head back and pour some water into my mouth. Not enough to keep me hydrated, but just enough to wash the bread down.

"We've come up with a great plan, and your friend Hope will be joining you here shortly." The boyfriend laughs.

My mind starts racing. I have to get out of here, but all that keeps flashing through my mind is if they take Hope, at least Cash will come for her since no one's coming for me.

A voice in my head reminds me that if Hope knew I was here, she and Cash would come after me in an instant. It's not unusual for us to go several days without talking, so they won't be missing me yet.

"Alright, doll, it's time for you to take another nap." The boyfriend reaches into his bag.

Thankfully, when they drugged me, they only used a needle that first time. Ever since, they've been putting something in the water they give me. It tastes disgusting, but I'm pretty sure it's sleep medication—a strong dose that works whether I want it to or not.

When he's done mixing, he looks at me and smiles. Thank God for small miracles—at least they're not torturing me today.

"Drink up, doll. When you wake up, your friend will be here. Won't that be a treat?" he asks in an overly excited voice.

I don't want to drink, but this isn't something worth fighting them on. I do as I'm told, and the room grows hazy before it goes black.

The next time I open my eyes, there's a chair a few feet away. Hope is strapped to it with her hands taped behind her back.

"Hope, wake up!" I call.

We're alone, and if we can get out of our bindings, we might have a chance.

"Hope!" I call again, but this time it brings her mom and the boyfriend from outside.

"Shut up, you mangy bitch," the boyfriend growls.

He takes something from his bag, and before I know it, he's shoving the cloth into my mouth and tying it behind my head.

Dammit.

All I can do is sit and wait until Hope wakes up. It seems like forever before she starts to stir, and when she opens her eyes, she's looking right at me. I try to convey everything with a look, but I don't think she understands me.

"Shit," she whispers.

I almost roll my eyes because that's an understatement.

She starts moving around, trying to free her arms and legs, which are bound like mine.

"Oh, good, you're awake." Her mom steps into the room and shoves a gag into Hope's mouth.

My mom had her issues, but good Lord, what kind of mom treats her daughter like this? As she shoves the gag into her mouth, Hope tries to yell out. I don't blame her. I'd fight every step of the way too, and I did.

"Told you to do this the easy way, and none of this would have happened," her mom says in a fake disappointed voice, making my stomach churn. She has no right to be disappointed in anybody right now.

"So, you're both probably wondering about the plan now, aren't you?" the boyfriend asks.

I don't know his name, nor do I care to learn it.

"If you'd handed over the money when your mother asked the first time, we would've taken it and been on our merry little way. We would've been in Mexico now, and you never would've heard from us again. But since you refused and moved so rudely without a forwarding address, we had to use your friend here to figure out where you were. That part wasn't too hard, as you might have guessed. I've had eyes on you for a long time."

The footprints at the edge of the woods that Cash was tracking were him? I know it was driving Cash and Hope nuts figuring out who was watching them at the cabin, and then all of a sudden, the footprints disappeared. Hope thought it was some hiker, especially since the one picture they got on the hunting camera was of a guy in a sweatshirt.

Looking at the boyfriend now, I guess I can see the resemblance.

"Of course, I was a little sloppy, and it made it hard to find a way to get you alone. That's where your friend here came in. We were going to use her as bait to get you out here by yourself. The perfect opportunity opened up today when we saw you were alone." He smiles that creepy smile as he starts to eat whatever food he's made.

"Now that we have you, we'll ransom you to your mega-rich boyfriend, and for a bonus price, he can also have your friend here." Her mom smiles. If you didn't know any better, you'd think it was one of those 1950s housewife smiles.

"I think we'll wait till tomorrow to make the call. Let him sweat it out. I bet we get more money for her that way," the boyfriend says as he walks over and pulls the gag from Hope's mouth.

"It's hilarious you two think you're going to make it out of this alive," Hope says with an evil smile.

Her smile is met with a slap across the cheek from the boyfriend, but she doesn't even flinch. It's like she felt nothing, and her smile doesn't falter. I've never seen this side of Hope before, but she's one bad bitch.

"You're the biggest piece of shit I've ever met and the most horrible mother. You can't die from a drug overdose soon enough," Hope spits at her mom before the boyfriend slaps her on the other side of her face. Again, she barely flinches.

"I raised you, and you owe me at least this," her mother says.

"I owe you for what? Starving me?" Her mother slaps her this time, but Hope stays strong.

That's also when the front door bursts open as someone slams into it. Cash bursts in with his dog, Hank, right on his heels. "Lay another hand on her, and I will kill you both."

I knew Cash would come for Hope. They have a bond, a connection. There's no doubt they're soulmates. They're meant to be together, and there's no way he would let them take Hope without a fight.

Before anyone can speak, the back door bursts open, and three large men step through. Cash's friend Axel is first, who detains Hope's mom by slamming her to the floor with a knee in her back.

Next comes Bennett, another of Cash's mountain men friends, who tackles the boyfriend in much the same way.

Another man walks in behind him, who I've never met. He has a big scar on the side of his face. Cash, Axel, and Bennett are tight, and if they trust this man, I will too.

He walks in and scans the room until he sees me. His eyes lock on mine, and it's like that moment everyone describes where time seems to stand still, and there's nothing but him and me in the room. Even though I'm still strapped to a chair and in pain, it disappears when his intense gaze is on me.

He breaks eye contact, and his gaze runs over the rest of my body. Taking a few steps across the room, he stops in front of me and drops to his knees. He gently removes the gag from my mouth and pulls a knife from his boot to cut my legs free. He reaches behind me and cuts the tape from my arms. His hands are gentle, helping my arms move around my body and placing my hands in my lap.

"The cops are on the way. I'll check their bag and see if we can figure out what they gave them," Axel says once Hope's mom and the boyfriend are tied up and can't move.

The man whose name I still don't know runs his hands up and down my arms as if he's trying to warm me up. The more he does it, the more the sensation returns to my arms.

I'm aware of people talking around me, but I hear nothing of what they're saying while this man's hands are on me. After a moment, he stands up and offers his hand to me. I take it and try to stand up for the first time in days, but the moment I put weight on my legs, they give out. Pain shoots up my leg from where the boyfriend took a bat to my ankle.

The mountain man wastes no time picking me up bridal style and looking over at Cash. "Let's take them to the road and wait for the cops. That way, they don't have to be around these two."

Cash nods, and just like that, this Hulk of a mountain man carries me out of the cabin. I have no idea what his name is, but I feel safer with him than I have in a long time.

That's the moment I realize I'm in trouble.

Chapter 2

Cole

I moved to the mountains to be away from people—all people. I won't go into town, and I don't have friends. The only person who knows I'm here is my neighbor Cash because we've run into each other a few times since my property borders his.

So, when there's a knock on the door, there's not a single person I'm expecting. I grab my shotgun, fully intent on having to put a bullet through whoever is standing on the other side of the door.

So, you can only imagine my shock when I open the door and find my neighbor, Cash.

"I don't know exactly what you did in the military, but I know you're a damn good tracker, and I need your help. Someone just kidnapped my girl, and the cops aren't doing anything. There are tracks, and there's blood. I have two other guys who are willing to help. From the looks of it, two people took her. We're going in, and I could use another man."

Fuck.

An innocent civilian involved in a kidnapping is not something I can ignore. I close the door and head straight to my office, where I keep a go backpack. I grab a couple of extra guns that I stash on me and put an extra pocket knife in my other boot before grabbing my semi-automatic gun and heading back out front.

I hop on my four-wheeler and follow Cash back to his place. I may not have friends, but I will say I don't mind Cash. He doesn't ask a lot of questions, which is great because I don't have a lot of answers to give him.

When I walk into his cabin, I'm greeted by three other men and two women. This is a lot for me, especially as it's been more than a year since I talked to anyone other than Cash.

"This is Cole. He's my neighbor and one of the best trackers I've ever seen. Cole, this is Axel and his wife, Emelie. Phoenix, and his wife, Jenna, and Bennett. They all live on the mountain. Phoenix is staying behind with the girls because if Hope were to get away, this is the first place she would come to find me."

Cash shows me around his place. The back door has been busted in, and there are signs of a struggle on the front porch, along with blood. Three sets of footprints become two sets, and the track marks indicate they probably knocked out the victim, who I know is a female.

Having all the information, I nod before I speak for the first time. "Let's go."

My military training kicks in as they grab their stuff. Two guys hop on the four-wheelers, and Cash walks with me as we track the footprints back to a dirt road. Looks like they got into a car, and with the rain we had last night, the tire tracks are pretty easy to trace. They go about a mile up the road and pull into what looks like an abandoned driveway.

"Any idea what's up there?" I ask, nodding up the driveway.

"No, but a few hunting cabins are scattered along this road. Most of them are abandoned now," Cash says.

We leave the four-wheelers on the road and continue on foot, sticking to the trees and following the driveway. The car tracks are clearly marked and lead to the long-abandoned cabin. It looks like a small one-room cabin with one bedroom in the back.

I pull out my binoculars and try to get a look into the house. That's when I find not one but two young women being detained. My gut churns, telling me that this mission is different, more important than any I've done in my life. I don't know how that's possible, considering I've worked some serious undercover classified missions, but I always trust my gut.

"Two young women are being detained, both tied to chairs," I tell them.

"Two?" Cash asks.

"There's a female standing in the room and a male entering from a back door also now in the room," I say before handing the binoculars to Cash.

"Fuck. The one on the right is my Hope, and the one on the left is her best friend, Jana. I'm pretty sure the female is her mom, but I have no idea who the guy is," Cash says.

The guys talk a bit about Hope and her mom as I formulate a plan in my head.

"Both Hope and Jana seem to be knocked out. They probably drugged them, so they were easier to manipulate. If they drugged her when they took her, she should be waking up anytime now unless they plan to keep her out for what-ever reason," Cash says.

"We need the girls awake, if possible, especially if the two holding them are drugged up. There's no telling how irrational they'll be or what kind of strength they might have," Axel says.

"Possible motive?" I ask, wanting to have all the information.

"Hope's mom was asking for money. My guess is they need to fund their drug problem. There's a possibility they could be on the run from something. They have misdemeanor backgrounds from what Hope knows," Cash says.

It all comes down to money. It always does. One way or another, they need money for this or that. If they're drug users, there's no telling what their reaction to anything will be, which makes them unpredictable and downright dangerous.

I circle the building, getting the lay of the land. As we wait for the girls to wake up, we talk and formulate our plan and get ready to head in. Cash and the dog go through the front as a distraction while the guys and me go through the back.

The plan works perfectly. Axel and Bennett have the male and female detained almost instantly. But the moment I step into the room and my eyes lock on the girl sitting next to Hope, the whole world tilts on an axis.

My gut tells me this girl is mine. Mine to take. Mine to protect.

I walk over and kneel in front of her, gently cutting through the tape binding her feet and arms to the chair.

Her arms are so limp that I gently lift them forward to her lap. They're ice cold, so I run my hands up and down her arms to get the blood circulating again. Unfortunately, this will also bring back any pain.

The guys talk all around me, but I hear none of it. I'm focused on this gorgeous, strong woman in front of me. She's staring at me, but it's at *me,* not my scar, and that alone is doing strange things to my heart.

I help the woman to stand, but her legs give out instantly. I catch her before she hits the ground with an arm under her legs and another under her shoulders, carrying her bridal style.

"Let's take them to the road and wait for the cops. That way, they don't have to be around these two," I say, and Cash nods.

"We got them. They're not going anywhere," Bennett says, nodding at the two detained on the floor.

I waste no time getting her away from them and heading up the driveway. The moon gives enough light to see where I'm going along the driveway where the trees aren't as thick.

She doesn't talk the whole way, but I can feel her eyes on me. Once we reach the road, I set her down on one of the four-wheelers as we wait for the cops.

"Are you okay?" Hope asks Jana.

I'm irrationally upset that her best friend asked her if she was okay before I was able to.

"Yeah, I.." She stops and coughs.

I pull a bottle of water from my backpack and hand it to her. She drinks it thirstily.

"Slow down. Small sips, or you'll throw it back up," I tell her.

She looks at me with wide eyes before doing as I ask.

I pull a protein bar from my backpack and hand it to her. "This isn't going to taste great, but it's got protein and some other things that will help you feel better."

She takes it from me. "I was taken the night I saw you guys. They grabbed me before I walked into my apartment," she says, taking a bite. "He kept asking me all sorts of questions about you. They wanted me to call and try to get you to meet me somewhere so they could get you away from Cash. I kept refusing. When I refused, they punished me, thinking the pain would change my mind. But you're my friend, and I wouldn't turn on you like that. Not for anything."

Hope gets up on wobbly legs and walks over to her. I take a step back and allow her to embrace her friend. An irrational feeling comes over me that I should be the one offering her comfort, but I push it back and let her and Hope have their moment.

When this beautiful girl starts crying, I almost push Hope out of the way to comfort her.

"I wouldn't have blamed you if you had done what they asked. I'd rather you stay alive. I don't know what I would do if I had lost you," Hope says.

It makes her cry harder, and she just sits there hugging Hope as my gut twists with every tear that falls.

"I had no one to come for me. When I saw you were, I was relieved because I knew Cash would come for you, and I'd finally be saved." She cries even harder.

I want to tell her that I will come for her. From this moment on, she will always have someone to come for her. But the words stick in my throat.

"You have me. Cash and I were going to check on you after he got done with his traps today. We would have realized something was wrong. I would have come for you," Hope says.

They hug for a moment longer before Hope steps away, and Cash places her back on the four-wheeler. I move in front of her, and she looks up at me with questions in her eyes.

"This is my neighbor, Cole. This is Hope's best friend, Jana," Cash introduces us.

I open my backpack, pull out another protein bar, and hand it to Cash for Hope. Then I check Jana's wounds, starting with her swollen ankle. I'm pretty sure it's sprained as she can move it.

She has a few cuts on her arms and what looks like a burn mark. There are some scratches on her face and a decent size cut at her temple that looks fresh. It's going to need stitches.

"Can I lay down and sleep until the cops get here?" Jana asks.

"No, you have a head wound, and I need you to stay awake. You're going to need stitches, and it needs to get cleaned up. When did you get this cut?" I tap her temple.

"Earlier today, right before they left. They gave me another dose of whatever they were using to knock me out. When I woke up, Hope was there, and they were back."

It's then the cops show up. I don't know how long they take, but they ask them both a bunch of questions and take pictures of their wounds. They also ask Cash and me a bunch of questions, which makes me uneasy, but I know it has to be done for the girls to be safe. They take notes before heading down the driveway to the cabin.

"You can bring her back to my place. We'll take care of her and get her to a hospital." Cash says to me.

"No, I can't go to the hospital. I don't have medical insurance. I can't afford to go." Jana starts to panic,

I instinctively cup her cheek, tilting her head to look at me. "I have medic training. You can stay with me. I'll stitch you up and get you all taken care of."

Jana looks over at Cash and Hope. She doesn't know me, and I'm sure she's wondering if she can trust me. It's good that she's hesitant. I would expect nothing less after what she's been through.

"He's a good guy. I trust him. And we'll be by to check on you. He lives not too far from me. You okay with that?" Cash asks Jana.

Jana looks back at me. Her eyes are like the sun breaking through a bank of clouds. She nods, confirming that she feels safe enough to come back to my place.

I turn her on the four-wheeler and get her situated before climbing on behind her. I wrap one arm around her waist and hold her snugly to me. Her body pressed against me has my cock as hard as nails for the first time in years, and there's no hiding it from her.

We say our goodbyes and head off. I keep my arm firmly around her, trying to be gentle and careful of her wounds. I could move my large hand a few inches in either direction to touch her tits or pussy, which I'd love to get my hands on.

This woman is going to be trouble in the best possible way.

Chapter 3

Jana

I'm aware of every inch of his skin touching me. From how his thighs cradle me to his hand touching every inch of skin below my bra to the top of my pants and his hard cock pressing against my back.

After everything that's happened, how the hell am I getting turned on?

The longer we ride on the four-wheeler and the further we get from that damn cabin, the safer I start to feel. The safer I feel, the more I relax, and the more I relax, the more pain I feel.

After a bit, I feel every little bump. Every time my foot gets jostled, it hurts, shooting pain up my leg, and my head is pounding.

"Hold on, firecracker. Only a few more minutes," he rumbles in my ear. He slows down over the bumps, trying to make it more bearable.

By the time we get to his cabin, I'm considering racking up a hospital bill just for some morphine to knock me out, even if it means working the rest of my life to pay the bill.

His cabin is exactly what I would expect—situated in the middle of the woods on a cleared piece of land. There are different outbuildings and a small garden.

He parks the four-wheeler by the front door before stepping off and gently lifting me into his arms to carry me inside. I'm expecting more of a bachelor pad-style cabin, but what we step into is something more out of a fancy magazine.

Most of the furniture looks to be handmade and custom-made for the space. It all perfectly matches with beautiful details. There are animal skin rugs and blankets, but they fit into this space like they were purchased from an expensive design store instead of handmade by the owner himself.

There's a large stone chimney, and I'm willing to bet the stones were picked right from his property. I don't get to look at anything else because he takes me back to the bathroom and sets me on the beautifully cold counter.

"I need to remove your clothes to check for other wounds," he says.

I hesitate. As safe as I feel with him and as turned on as I was a little while ago, my first thought is not to take all my clothes off in front of him.

"And your clothes need to be cleaned," he adds like he's trying to convince me to do as he asks.

"And what do you suggest I wear in the meantime?" I ask because walking around his house with no clothes is not an option.

He looks at me for a moment and then disappears from the bathroom without a word. Does he expect me to follow him? Maybe if I had crutches, but there's no way I'm walking on this ankle.

He's back a moment later with some of his clothes.

"Those are going to be huge on me," I say as he sets them on the counter next to me.

"Let's start with your pants so I can get a good look at your ankle." He gently removes my shoes and socks before looking back up at me.

I nod and unbutton my jeans, bracing myself on the counter and lifting my butt so he can gently pull the jeans down my legs.

He looks nervous and tense, and I get a pang of pleasure at being able to throw him off his usual calm and sure demeanor.

My right ankle is noticeably bruised, cut, and heavily swollen. He gently runs his hands over me, checking my flexibility and making sure I can move my toes and ankle before letting out a string of curses under his breath.

"I'm pretty sure it's just sprained. You should have it looked at, but I'll clean it up, we'll get some ice on it, and then I'll wrap it up. You'll have to stay off this for at least a few days. Even then, it's going to be painful to walk."

He opens the cabinet under the sink and pulls out a bunch of first aid items, cleaning every little cut and scratch. When he's done with my legs, he helps me remove my shirt. Thankfully, he allows me to leave my bra and underwear on.

He treats and wraps the burn on my arm and my other scratches before turning his attention to my face. "This is going to need stitches," he says, looking at my temple.

"Please tell me you have some kind of numbing medication," I almost beg him. "Despite how brave you might think I am, I'm a chicken when it comes to needles."

His eyes are still on the cut, but he smirks a little.

"Glad to know that I can at least amuse you," I say when he doesn't answer me.

"I have something that will do, but it won't ease the pain completely," he says, disappearing from the bathroom again.

He's back seconds later with a blanket and wraps it around me before leaving the room to get whatever numbing medication he has on hand. I hear cabinets open and close in the kitchen before he comes back into the bathroom.

"Drink a little bit of this. A little bit will go a long way since you haven't eaten." He hands me a bottle of whiskey.

"This is your pain medication?" I take the bottle and stare at it.

"No, this is, but the whiskey will ease whatever this doesn't cover." He holds up a little bottle that looks like an antiseptic cream from the first aid kit.

He washes his hands again and gently applies the cream. Even the slightest touch of his finger hurts. I try to be brave, but I take a big swig of the whiskey the first chance I get.

It burns on the way down and instantly warms my body. I'm not a big whiskey drinker. I prefer fruity cocktails, but I've never been as thankful for whiskey as I am now.

"So, what is it that you do that you don't have health insurance?" he asks as he starts getting everything ready to stitch up the cut on my temple.

"I run the grocery store and cafe in town," I tell him and take another smaller sip of the whiskey.

"Surely you qualify for some self-employment insurance," he says as he gets to work on the cut.

"I don't own the places. The general manager is a decent guy, but he works around the government. Each is a separate business, and he pays for my room and board in the apartment above the café. Technically, I have two jobs, but neither one quite qualifies for healthcare and benefits, although my income is more than decent." I recite what I've told my mom multiple times. She thinks I should look for something else, but I love my apartment and my life here.

"That doesn't sound like a good guy to me."

"Well, if you only look at it that way, yeah. But as far as bosses go, he's one of the best I've worked for. He trusts me to run the place and stays out of it as long as I send him the monthly reports and things add up. I'm not in a position to rock the boat just yet." I take another swig of whiskey,

I don't feel any pain, just some pressure and a little bit of tugging. As long as I don't think about what he's doing, it doesn't make my stomach roll.

"Where did you get all this training to be able to take care of me and stitch me up?" I ask, wanting to know more about him.

"The military," he says almost absentmindedly before he steps back and indicates he's done.

"I don't suppose you're going to elaborate on your military time, are you?" I ask as he starts cleaning things off and putting everything away.

"Nope." One simple gruff word.

He looks like a mountain man. Rough around the edges, beard, his hair on the long side, and needing a cut. His clothes are worn, and tattoos and scars cover his arms. The scar on his face makes him look intimidating, but he was so gentle, taking care of my ankle and stitching me up.

Once everything is put away, he picks up the shirt he brought in earlier. "If you take the rest of your clothes off, I'll get them washed so they can dry. The shirt should be big enough for you. Keep the blanket. It'll keep you warm," he says before turning and leaving the room.

I don't know if he's coming back, so I quickly slip my bra and underwear off before putting his shirt on. The shirt is like a dress on me, although it leaves my legs bare.

With the sun already set, the temperature outside will drop quickly this time of year. I wrap the blanket around me and figure out how I'm going to get out to the living room. There seems to be enough furniture I could balance myself on and hop around on one foot.

"Are you dressed?" his deep voice fills the bathroom, but he's standing in the doorway where he can't see me.

"Yes."

He enters the room without another word, picks me up, and carries me out to the living room.

"You know I'm going to have to figure out how to get around at some point. You're going to get sick of caring for me everywhere," I tell him as he sets me down on the couch.

I'm not a thin girl by any means. I work in a cafe, and I like my cupcakes and donuts. I think the last time I had a thigh gap was in elementary school, and I have to hit the plus size section to find clothes. My job keeps me somewhat in shape because of all the walking between the two stores. I tell myself the weight is mostly muscle, but it's still weight, and I know he can tell every time he picks me up.

"You weigh nothing. I'll carry you until your foot heals," he grunts and turns to the kitchen.

I sit there shocked. It's like he was reading my mind. "Are you a mind reader?"

He pauses, looking through the refrigerator to look back at me. "It was written all over your face. Out here, it's a good thing you're not all sticks and bones," he says before pulling some stuff out of the refrigerator.

The living room, dining room, and kitchen are open-plan. It's cozy with the fire crackling in the fireplace. I'm not sure when he started it, but I'm thankful he did.

He joins me again after a few minutes. "I'm warming up some leftovers. You'll eat and drink this," he says, handing me a cup of water.

I take it from him and keep my mouth shut because now is not a good time to remind him he should be asking instead of telling. I drink the water and realize I'm thirstier than I thought when I hand him back an empty glass. He nods approvingly before heading to the kitchen to refill it, and this time I sip it.

"How long have you lived here?" I ask, wanting to fill the silence.

"A while."

OK, let me try another subject to get him talking. "Did you build this cabin yourself?"

"Yes."

Such a conversationalist. I keep quiet and look around until the timer goes off and he brings me my food. It looks like a roast with potatoes, carrots, and gravy. He sits on the couch beside me with his plate. I hesitantly take a small bite, only to discover this is one of the best meals I've had in a long time.

"Your prior military, with pretty good medic experience. A mountain man who builds cabins. And you can cook. What other surprises am I going to find out about you?" I ask jokingly.

"I have plenty of surprises for you once you're feeling better, firecracker," he says, only he's not joking.

Chapter 4

Cole

"No! Don't touch me! Stop!" a voice in obvious distress pulls me from sleep.

I'm ready to interfere and protect the woman who needs help until I realize she's lying in bed next to me. Jana is having a nightmare, and from the sounds of it, it's about her ordeal at the cabin.

I turn over and gently rub her arm.

"Jana, you're safe. You're not there anymore. You're safe with me." I repeat the words as I gently try to wake her up.

Her eyelids flutter, and when she opens her eyes, they're full of confusion. "Cole?"

"Yeah. You were having a nightmare."

She groans and turns to face me. She plasters herself to my side, resting her head on my shoulder and tangling her legs with mine while wrapping her arm over my chest.

I tense. Sharing a bed with Jana was already outside my comfort zone, but she didn't want to be left alone and refused to let me sleep on the couch. My bed is big enough that I'd have been fine if we each stayed to our sides. But having her wrapped around me like this is a little too much.

"Let me get you a glass of water," I say, trying to get out of bed.

"No!" She sounds almost panicked as she clings to me tighter.

She's panicked at the thought of me leaving. If her nightmare took her back to that cabin, being inside might be the last thing she needs right now.

"OK, then you'll come with me." I don't give her time to respond. I wrap the blanket around her and scoop her up in my arms.

I take her to the kitchen and set her on the counter while I get her a glass of water. Then I scoop her up again and head out to the back porch. I sit in one of the Adirondack styles chairs I built and arrange her on my lap.

"The sun should be coming up. We'll sit out here as long as you want," I tell her.

"Thank you, Cole." She rests her head on my shoulder and snuggles into me as she slowly relaxes.

"After everything I saw in the military, I'd wake up many nights, and it would take me minutes to realize where I was. Sitting here watching the sunrise over the mountains was a great reminder that I was safe," I confess. As uncomfortable as I am sharing, I know it's what she needs.

She tried earlier to get me to open up before she shut down. I don't like her shutting down. I want to know every little detail about her, but I get the feeling she won't share with me if I don't open up to her.

"This is perfect," she says.

Neither of us moves as we watch the first hints of the sun peek over the mountain tops. With any luck, the sky will burst into beautiful colors for her to enjoy up here. It's usually pinks and purples and some reds during sunrise.

"I'm not... it's not easy to talk about myself. I haven't had to for many years," I admit, breaking the silence.

"It's okay. I understand. You moved out here for a reason, and it wasn't because you wanted a social life."

She gets me. If that isn't even more reason to at least try for her, I don't know what is.

"I want to tell you. Not everything because there are things from my military time that don't need to touch you, but I want you to know me," I admit.

She sits up and looks at me like she did in the bathroom. She looks at *me*, not at my scar, making me feel seen.

"After I was injured in the military, I went to a place called Oakside. It's a military rehab facility that helps injured veterans transfer into civilian life and heal after their time in the hospital." I start slowly as she snuggles back into me. She doesn't push but lets me tell her at my own pace.

"Noah and his wife, Lexi, run the place. During his time in the military, he was badly injured with burns on one side of his body, including his face. It made it easier knowing I wasn't the only one permanently scarred. But it didn't make it any less noticeable."

I try to shut down all the old feelings so I can tell her my story, at least part of it.

"It didn't stop the stares and the questions. Most people wouldn't say anything. They knew my scars were militarily related. But they stared, and people looked at me differently, especially the visitors who came to visit their loved ones. A few kids cried when they saw me. Eventually, I stopped trying and moved out here. It was easier, and I felt safer out here."

"If people looked at you differently, that's their problem, not yours, and you shouldn't alter your life because of them," she says, sounding upset about the whole situation.

"You and the other mountain men are the first people who haven't looked at me differently in years," I tell her.

She for my hand. Something about her small hand in my big one pulls my heartstrings. Then it hits me. Now she's all fixed up, she might want to go home. With the help of crutches, she could get around on her own and go back to work. But I'm not ready for her to leave.

If I have to guess, tonight won't be her last nightmare. Which gives me an idea.

"With everything you've been through in the last few days, I think it's best you're not left alone. You should stay here where I can monitor your ankle and tend to your cut to make sure there are no infections, at least until the stitches are ready to come out," I say, hopeful she won't push the issue. Hopefully, she'll understand I don't want her to go.

"I think that's for the best. I'm not in any rush to be alone anyway," she says.

We sit in silence and watch the sun finish rising.

"Do you like blueberry muffins?" I ask her once the sun is finally filling the sky.

"Yes, they're my go-to breakfast in the mornings when I work at the café."

I tuck that piece of valuable information away, knowing it'll be important later. I want to know everything about her, so the more she feels comfortable telling me, the better.

"There are some blueberry bushes in the tree line over there. There should be enough ripe ones ready to be picked. Wait here, and I'll get some and make us breakfast." I stand and place her back in the chair.

Jana nods but watches my every move. I head inside for a moment to put my shoes on, and as I walk to the tree line, I can feel her eyes on my back.

Usually, the feeling of someone watching me makes me extremely uneasy and puts me on edge, but knowing her eyes are on me is comforting. I like knowing she's there waiting for me, and I get to take care of her.

I get to the tree line and start checking the bushes. It's not peak picking time yet, but there's plenty ripe to make enough muffins for breakfast. I start picking, all my thoughts focused on the fact that I got her to agree to stay at least for a few days.

I want to show her about life out here. Heck, she's friends with Cash and his girl, so she has to know a bit about life out here. Has she thought about living out here herself? Maybe I can get her to spend some time with me and see that she could fit in here because I hate the thought of her leaving.

When I have enough blueberries, I turn to head back and realize I'm out of eyesight of her. As I emerge into the clearing from the woods, I can tell something is wrong.

I take off and run straight to her to find her having what looks like a panic attack.

"Jana. I'm right here. Take a deep breath in, slow and steady."

Her eyes lock on mine, and she does as I ask.

"Now breathe out. Slowly in through your nose, count to five, then slowly breathe out through your mouth, counting to five. Focus on me." I try to distract her and get her to slow her breathing.

After a few rounds of counting each breath, she seems to be back in control.

"I... I couldn't..." she takes another deep breath in and out. "I couldn't see you... then I couldn't breathe," she says before trying to take another deep breath.

After everything that she's been through, panic attacks aren't surprising. I'm beyond ecstatic that she sees me as safe, even if I hate that she has to deal with this.

"I promise not to leave your side again." My protective instinct kicks in now to protect her from anything and everything, even if it means she's glued to my side until she feels safe again.

Chapter 5

Jana

How is it possible to feel so safe with someone you just met?

I've never had a panic attack before, but when he ventured further into the woods and I couldn't see him, my mind played tricks on me. I imagined Hope's mom and the boyfriend trying to kidnap me all over again, dragging me back to that cabin.

But he knew what to do. He was right there to pull me out of it. Focusing on him when I couldn't catch my breath calmed me in a way no one's been able to do.

Now sitting at his kitchen island watching him make blueberry muffins, it all seems so normal. Like my time in that cabin is a million miles away and can't touch me here.

How badly I want that to be true.

I was surprised last night to find out that Cole can cook and cook well. But I guess that shouldn't be too surprising. The mountain men out here have to take care of themselves. After all, it's not like they can pop into the diner every night for dinner. If you want decent food, you have to know how to make it yourself.

"How do you know Hope and Cash?" Cole asks as he starts making breakfast.

He may not talk much, but he seems to like me talking. I notice he's asking me questions and listens intently to what I have to say. I would have thought he'd be more of a silent man and wouldn't want me filling that silence.

So as long as he wants me to talk, I will because when the silence kicks in is when I start to overthink everything that's happened.

"Hope started coming into the cafe and sat in the area attached to the grocery store. She broke out a computer and started working using the free Internet. After seeing her there day after day, I finally approached her and introduced myself. We started talking every time she came in and slowly bonded. She was new in town."

She may not be the friend I've known the longest, but I'd consider her my best friend.

She's a better friend than the people I knew at high school, despite her mother being cuckoo crazy. Thankfully, that doesn't run in the family.

"A few months ago, she met Cash. He came into the store after his brother died, and she helped him find what he needed. They bonded. I got to know him as they started dating. He's always accepted me as part of Hope's life, even when my ex treated him like crap."

I frowned, remembering that ill-fated game day where I tried to get Cash to bond with my ex-boyfriend, Alex. It caused a huge fight between not only Hope and Cash but Hope and me. That led to a huge fight between Alex and me that caused us to break up, allowing me to see him for the asshole he was.

"Ex-boyfriend?" Cole asks when I stop talking.

"Yeah. It was Cash who helped me see what an asshole he was. Even if we were still together, I doubt he'd even notice I was missing. He was my longest relationship, just under two years."

I don't know why I told him that or why I'm oversharing because he doesn't seem to like me talking about my ex.

"Hope and Cash introduced me to the other men and their wives, and I fit in better with them than with my friends in town. So I tend to hang out with them more even though we don't get together near as much."

Oddly enough, that seems to make him relax. I'm not going to pretend that I understand mountain men.

"Working at the only grocery store in town, I've seen and met everybody, but I haven't seen you. Why?"

If he's been here several years, as he says, I should have seen him in town, at least for some of the basics. Even the most remote mountain men still order flour and sugar and stuff in a bulk order and pick it up once a year.

Cole tilts his head so his scar is facing me as if to say, *Are you serious? How did you miss this?*

He's saying he hasn't been in town to pick up supplies because of his scar? Without thinking, I stand and use the counter to hobble along, keeping the weight off my injured foot. I don't stop until I'm standing in front of him.

I reach up and gently place my fingers on his chin, turning his head again so his scar Is facing me. I can tell he's tense, but he doesn't stop me. Moving slowly so he knows my intent, I reach up and trace the scar on his face.

His hands remain at his side, but he squeezes them into fists. He's uncomfortable, but I meant what I said earlier. If someone doesn't like his scar, it's their problem, not his.

I trace his scar from the tip of his eyebrow, across his cheek, and down his jaw. When I start to slowly trace back up, he reaches and gently wraps his hand around my wrist. He holds my hand and turns his head slightly, placing a kiss on my palm.

His soft lips may be on my hand, but I feel them everywhere. As his lips leave my skin, his eyes lock on mine as his other hand wraps around my waist, gently pulling me closer.

When his head leans down toward me, there's no shadow of a doubt that he's going to kiss me. I've never wanted a kiss so bad in my life. My heart races because if this kiss is anything like the sensation of his lips on my hand, I'll never be the same.

When his lips land on mine, my head starts to spin. He slides his hand from my waist around my lower back. He grips the shirt I'm wearing like he is trying hard to be gentle with me when it's not in his nature. He takes a step forward and presses us together with no space between us.

His erection presses into my belly, and it's sexy as hell. His lips are soft and hesitant, but there's no mistaking that he's the one in control. His other hand releases my wrist and cups the back of my head, pulling me closer. His tongue traces my lips; I'm so wet, I can feel it dripping down my thighs. I've never been this turned on by a kiss in my life.

I'm about to get even closer when he pulls back. Only then do I hear the oven timer going off. His eyes linger on me before he looks at the oven and turns it off. He opens it but then turns back to me.

He wraps both hands around my waist and sets me on the kitchen counter in one quick move. I can see the silent warning in his look to stay off my ankle. Once I'm settled on the counter, he turns back the muffins and pulls them out of the oven.

He sets the table before picking me up and carrying me to the chair. I feel like I should reiterate that I can get there myself, but I like having his hands on me, so I keep my mouth shut.

"What do you like about living in town?" Cole asks after I take my first bite of food.

"I like the people. My job allows me to see people regularly. I like being downtown, close to the community garden I set up. My apartment isn't that bad. The smells of baking from the cafe drift up, so I don't ever have to buy fufu scented candles. I always smell like coffee and pastries, and my dog loves it."

I freeze, and my eyes go wide. "Shit! Muffin!" I panic about what a horrible dog mom I am after being kidnapped for several days. I forgot all about my dog when a hunky mountain man fell into my lap.

"Yes, you're eating a muffin?" he says, clearly confused.

"No, my dog is named Muffin. I forgot all about her. I'm such a horrible person. Who forgets about their dog? I have to go get her. She's been trapped in the house for days. Who knows what she's eating for food?"

"Calm down. It's perfectly understandable you wouldn't be thinking of anyone else in your situation," he tries to reassure me.

But my panic continues to rise, thinking my dog could be lying there, starving to death. Not to mention all the poop and pee that's probably covering my apartment. "No, you have to take me to her now. We have to go. She hasn't eaten in days or been outside. If someone calls animal control, they'll take her from me. I'll never get her back." I start to work myself into another full-blown panic attack.

He's up from his chair and in front of me in an instant. "Breathe in through your nose out through your mouth. Deep breaths." He works with me on my breathing again.

"You're in no shape to go anywhere. I'll go get your dog and bring her back here."

Chapter 6

Cole

I grip the steering wheel so hard my knuckles are white.

I've lived in Whiskey River for years, but I've never been into town, and now I'm driving down the mountain to go pick up Jana's dog.

Thankfully, I was able to get hold of Cash on the radio, and he and Hope came over to sit with Jana so she wouldn't be alone. Hope was thrilled because she wanted to check up on her anyway. When Cash learned where I was going, he gave me a look that I still don't quite understand— probably telling me I'm crazy for going into town, no matter how nice they are. One look at my scar is all it'll take to send people running.

I'm quickly finding that I don't care how many people I send running because there's nothing I won't do for her. I take that back—I won't move to town for her, but anything else is on the table.

As I'm driving down the mountain, all I can think about is that kiss. She's proven that my scar doesn't bother her in the slightest. It was my last worry, and now all bets are off. Whatever it takes to make her mine because I know without a shadow of a doubt that she was made for me.

I don't know what I'm walking into when I get to town or even her apartment. I follow her directions and pull around to the back of the café, parking next to her little blue four-door car.

My truck looks out of place in this parking lot. Thankfully, Axel found Jana's purse when the cops were going through everything in the cabin. He gave it to Cash, who brought it over before I left, so I have the keys to her apartment.

As I walk up the steps to the shared landing to the place next door, a little old woman is watching out the window, frowning at me. Wouldn't be surprised if she calls the cops. That'll be a great thing to have to explain. I offer her a friendly smile as I take the keys and head into the apartment.

The first thing I'm hit with is the stench of urine and feces. There's no denying a dog lives here. A dog food bag is spilled in the small kitchen area, and poop and pee cover the floor. The only thing missing is the dog.

"Muffin. Here girl." I try to sing a song to coax her from wherever she might be hiding.

When she doesn't make an appearance, I figure if I start to clean up, she'll eventually come out and see what's going on. I head to the kitchen and look for some trash bags and paper towels to start cleaning up the mess. Thankfully, the dog is small, as are the piles of poop.

Once that's done, I take the bag outside and across the parking lot to the dumpster. When I head back in, there's still no sign of muffin.

"What do you think you're doing, young man?" the old lady from the window next door stands in the doorway staring at me with her hands on her hips.

She's a tiny little thing, barely five feet tall. I'm well over six feet and could easily overpower her, yet she's standing here demanding to know what I'm doing. I smirk a little because I instantly like her.

"Jana ask me to get her dog. She seems to be hiding, so I thought I'd clean up in hopes of coaxing her out."

The woman just stands there looking at me. "Where is Jana?"

"She's at my place. She was injured, so she's resting."

This seems to soften the woman. "It's been a few days since Jana has been home. That dog has been howling up a storm. I have her spare keys, so I came over and got her. Come on."

Without waiting for me turns and heads back out the door. Again, I could easily overpower this woman, and here she is, inviting me into her house. I can't go back without the dog, so I don't have a choice as I follow her next door.

"Now sit down. I'm going to grab some tea and cookies, and I want to hear all about how Jana got hurt," she says and heads to the kitchen.

That's when a little puff of fur comes running out and starts circling and sniffing my legs. This little dog must be Muffin. She must smell Jana on me because she wags her tail a mile a minute.

I look around the living room to find a place to sit. The two small rocking chairs look like they'd crumble under my weight. I decide to take my chances with the pink floral couch and carefully sit on one side. The dog jumps up on the couch and settles right in my lap, trying to jump up and lick my face.

"It takes a good man to clean an apartment like that. In my day, men refused to clean, saying it was the woman's duty to do all the cleaning," the little lady says with a smile as she returns to the room.

Her place is better-lit than Jana's, so I'm expecting her to take one look at my scar and recoil or show some form of fear. But she doesn't even flinch. She sets the tray of cookies and tea on the coffee table and hands me my cup before filling hers and sitting down.

"Now, what happened to Jana?" she asks as she looks at me.

Again, I wait for a reaction but get nothing.

"A few nights ago, she was coming home after dark, and she was kidnapped. The same people who kidnapped her also took her friend Hope. I helped my neighbor, Cash, get them back."

"Good heavens! Who would do such a thing, especially here in Whiskey River?" she gasps.

"What are you rambling on about, Maisie?" another old lady walks into the house without knocking.

"This gentleman here was telling me how Hope and Jana were kidnapped. That's why she hadn't been here to take care of her dog," Maisie explains.

The other lady looks at me, and I expect her to jump or flinch, but I get none of that. She looks me over without letting her opinion show.

"And who is your young man?" she asks.

"I'm Cole. Jana is staying at my place while she heals."

I want to say I'm her boyfriend, and she's mine, but it doesn't seem like the place to start that conversation.

"And how do you know them?" She continues to grill me.

" Cash's girl, Hope, is my neighbor, Ms..."

"Mrs. Tipton. And how come we haven't seen you in town before?"

I guess this is a question I'll get often. I turn my head so my scars are in plain view.

"I'm waiting for an answer," she says, not taking the hint.

I point to the scar on my face.

She huffs and waves her hand at me. "That's no excuse to hide away. What qualifies you to take care of Jana instead of taking her to a hospital? And is Hope okay? Who kidnapped them?" Mrs. Tipton continues.

"If you give him a moment, he might answer your questions." Maisie sasses her friend.

"I have medic training from the military. Other than a sprained ankle and a cut that needed a few stitches, there was nothing major. She doesn't want to be alone right now, and that's going to take some time to get past. Hope is fine. A group of us rescued them when the cops wouldn't do anything. And it was Hope's mom and her mom's boyfriend who kidnapped her. They wanted money for drugs."

"My goodness. I heard her mom was here looking for her. If we'd known, we never would have been nice to that woman," Maisie says.

"I told you something was off about her," Mrs. Tipton says before she finally sits in the other rocking chair.

At this point, Muffin is exhausted from all the excitement and has decided I can be trusted because she's falling asleep in my lap. Patting her helps calm my nerves, so I don't mind.

"I wasn't surprised when Hope decided to move in with Cash. She seemed like she'd belong up there on the mountain, but I don't think Jana would be suited to life up there. She's so involved here between the community garden and the cafe and the grocery store. She likes talking and helping people," Maisie says, looking at me expectantly.

"I don't have any answers for you right now. I wish I did. All I know is Jana wants her dog. She's worried sick about her, and she needs to rest for a few more days at least." I tell them.

"I'll call the assistant manager and let them know. Jana's got nothing to worry about. The store and the cafe will be taken care of. Tell her to focus on rest, and I'll expect all the details when she gets back.

Both ladies get me everything I need, between the dog's food, toys, and the mat she likes to sleep on. I pass a few people in the parking lot, who look at me, but they don't seem disgusted by my scar.

On the way home, the whole encounter runs through my head. Not a single person seemed scared of the scar or disgusted by it. No one asked or pried into something I didn't want to discuss. I convince myself that it's just Whiskey River. This town is different. It's a small town, after all.

Then I think about what Maisie and Mrs. Tipton said about Jana. She's involved in the town.

She loves it there. Am I going to be able to convince her to move to the mountain with me after only knowing her for twenty-four hours? I have the added benefit of living next door to her best friend. Maybe Hope and Cash can help me convince her.

One thing I am sure of—my whole life is about to be turned upside down.

Chapter 7

Jana

Hope pulls me into a huge hug the moment she walks through the door. Cash didn't hide his shock when Cole told him he was going into town to get my dog. To be honest, I'm still a bit shocked and nervous.

"OK, tell me everything. Are you comfortable here? What's he like? Do you want to stay or come back with us? How are you feeling?" Hope fires off so many questions all at once.

"Love, give her a moment to answer your questions before asking new ones." Cash chuckles.

"I feel okay. Yes, I'm comfortable here. He's exactly how you would picture another mountain man, but he's nice too. I want to stay here for a little bit, but I reserve the right to change my mind." I don't want to worry them with the nightmares I've been having.

Hope glances at the stitches on the side of my head before looking into my eyes. "There's something else, isn't there?"

"Damn it, how can you read me like that?" I slump against the couch.

"It's a special skill you get when you're born in the South. Now spill."

"I had a nightmare last night about being back at the cabin and couldn't get back to sleep. Cole went out to pick some blueberries to make breakfast, I lost sight of him and had a panic attack. I've never had one before."

"You've just been through a traumatic experience, even more so than me. It's to be expected." Hope scoots closer to me on the couch and wraps her arm around my shoulders. "Do you like him?"

I could play stupid and pretend I don't know what she's talking about, but it would still come to the same answer. "Yes, I do."

"Good because him going to town to get your dog says everything. Cole has lived here for over five years and has never once been into town. You're with him for less than a day and got him to go," Cash says, shaking his head in disbelief.

I'm as shocked as he is.

"We both had a feeling about each other when we met. It just took us a little bit longer to get there," Hope says.

She and Cash lock eyes and smile as if re-membering when they first met, which was only a few months ago.

"Just remember, we're not far away, and we're happy to come to get you anytime, day or night," Cash says.

"We have news of our own." Hope squeals and bounces in her seat before holding her hand to show me a gorgeous diamond ring. "Cash proposed last night!"

I would be lying if I said I hadn't been expect-ing this. To be honest, I'm shocked Cash waited this long. A blind person could see how he feels about Hope, and she adores him.

"I'm so happy for you guys! Have you talked about plans and what you want to do?" I'm ex-cited for my friends, and it's good to focus on something other than the ordeal.

"We want a simple wedding here on the mountain. Something small with friends. Nei-ther of us has any family to invite. There are a few people in town, so we're going to have it by the cabin overlooking the mountains," Hope says, a beautiful glow on her face as she smiles at Cash.

The way he looks at her is every girl's dream. It's a look of pure love that says he'll do anything to make her happy.

My mind drifts back to Cole, who's down in town right now. He's making a huge sacrifice for me, and it's not something I take lightly.

"Once I'm back on my feet, I'd love to help out. I can decorate, cook, bake, you name it," I offer.

"I plan to take you up on that," Hope says, leaning over and hugging me.

"Cash and I are heading into town tomorrow, so we'll check on the community garden for you. Is there anything you need while we're down in town? Or anyone we need to talk to for you?"

"I could use some clothes. I called the assistant manager and asked her to take over for me while I'm here. And I spoke to the owner to let him know. I've been stocking up on sick days and vacation time, so I've got a few weeks before I need to worry about anything," I tell them.

"How did your boss take it?" Hope asks.

She's never been thrilled with my boss, who tries to get around things like health insurance, but she's supportive and has my back.

"He was concerned, especially when I told him I could get him a copy of the police report. He said it wasn't necessary, but once I get back into town, I'll stop and get a copy in case he changes his mind."

I try to ensure all my bases are covered, realizing how much of my life is committed back in town. The community garden runs solely based on the volunteers who help, but it's my baby and something I organize year after year.

My boss won't let me go too long without getting back to work. I know he'll let me use my vacation and sick days, but I don't have many options after that.

"Let me make you some lunch. Do you need ice for your ankle?" Hope starts asking questions, distracting me from my worries.

They stay with me until Cole returns, reminding me they're a phone call away whenever I'm ready to leave. I don't miss the little smirk Cash gives Cole on his way out. This big, bulky mountain man holding my tiny dog is a sight to see.

Once they leave, Cole brings Muffin over to me, who practically leaps from his arms into my lap. She licks my face and sniffs all over, paying special attention to my injured ankle.

"How bad is my apartment?"

Cole sits on the couch next to me. "Not bad now I cleaned it up. Your neighbor went in and got the dog. I guess she'd been barking. She asked about you. Her friend was there too and was concerned about Hope. I told them what happened but assured them you both were okay," he says as he watches me pet Muffin.

"I'm glad she took care of Muffin. I'm willing to bet the whole town knows what happened to Hope and me by now. Those two are the worst gossips." They're also the two women who keep me up to date on everything in Whiskey River, and I know I'll be peppered with questions as soon as I get home.

I can't believe Cole cleaned up my apartment, rescued Muffin, and talked to my neighbors. "I know it was a lot for you, and I appreciate it." I set Muffin down on the floor and scoot closer to him.

"They didn't flinch or even ask about my scar," he says as he watches my every move.

"If they have an issue with your scar, that's on them. Most people in Whiskey River won't give a shit about it. They care about you and the type of person you are."

"I see that now, even if spending too much time in town isn't in the cards for me."

I try not to think about his last statement because I'm so proud of him for taking the first steps. His actions speak volumes; I've never been this turned on by something so simple.

After sitting in his lap all morning while he held me after a nightmare, and the kiss we shared, I don't want to deny myself anymore. I want to show him how grateful I am, so I grab the front of his shirt and pull him toward me.

Cole comes without hesitation and wastes no time leaning in to kiss me. His kisses are so gentle compared to how rough he looks, and the contrast is intoxicating. I pull him with me as I slowly lie on the couch. He shifts his weight, bracing his weight on his arms over the top of me without breaking the connection of our lips.

"We have to stop," he whispers against my lips.

"Why?"

"Because if we don't stop now, I won't be able to. I'll taste every inch of you and take you here on the couch."

"That sounds like a horrible reason to stop, don't you think?"

He looks up at me. "You want this? Because I want you more than I want my next breath."

"I want you so much I don't think I'll live if you say we have to wait."

He wastes no time ripping our shirts off before leaning in to kiss me again. "This means you're mine, firecracker. And I'm yours. No going back."

That's all I want. Someone who loves me so much, he's willing to go into town to get my dog after not leaving his property for years. Someone strong enough to rescue me when I need it.

Cole carefully pulls down my sweat pants, rubbing his hard erection in the process. He groans, looking pained as he tries to control himself. He pulls my panties off and situates himself between my legs. I try to close them and pull him back up to me.

"Firecracker, I wasn't kidding when I said I was going to taste every inch of you."

"But... it's just..."

He pauses and looks up at me. "What is it?" he asks gently.

My face heats up. It's embarrassing to admit. I'd rather he drop it, but this is Cole, and he won't. Of course, he won't. "No one has done... that before." I try to convey my message without saying the words.

"No one has ever eaten every drop of cream from you as you came on their tongue?" he asks with a smirk.

I shake my head.

"Good." Then he dives in and latches on to my clit before he starts licking every inch of me.

Fuck, it feels good. The sensation of his tongue and the heat of his mouth. The harder I grip his hair, the more he seems to enjoy it. But when he thrusts a finger inside me, I lose it and come screaming his name.

Only when I relax does he kiss his way up my body. Somewhere along the line, he's removed the rest of his clothes. He leans in and kisses me again before pulling back to look into my eyes. He wants to know if I've changed my mind. I sure as hell haven't.

He grips my hips and slowly slides inside me. I suddenly remember I haven't taken my birth control pill since I was kidnapped. I should tell him, but all thoughts vanish when he slowly slides out and back into me.

"Fuck, you are so damn tight." He groans as he continues at a slow pace.

"Don't be gentle with me, Cole."

He nods and moves my hands above my head. He holds them in one of his, bracing a foot on the ground and starting a punishing pace.

He isn't gentle, but it's what I need after the last few days. Pure pleasure to wipe everything else away. He lets go of my wrists to play with my clit, already knowing how to bring me to the edge.

"Come for me, baby. You feel too good for me to last." He keeps up his pace as his eyes meet mine.

The intense emotion and the strength of our connection, combined with his mastery of my body, send me over the edge harder than before. He's right behind me, and with a shout of my name, his warm release fills me.

Cole shudders before finally sitting up and slowly pulling out of me. His eyes are locked between my thighs as his cum starts to slide out. He looks up, and his eyes meet mine like he's waiting for a reaction. I smile, and his eyes drop between my legs again. I gasp as he pushes his cum back into me before leaning in to kiss me.

"Let's get you a shower." He sweeps me into his arms and carries me to the bathroom.

Letting this man take care of me is becoming dangerously addictive.

Chapter 8

Cole

For the first time in my life, I feel truly content. My girl is in bed in my arms where she should be, and things are starting to look up. I had a feeling Whiskey River was going to be a special place, but I had no idea how much.

Jana looks so relaxed in bed. After our time on the couch last night, I took her to bed and worshiped her body all over again before she passed out from sheer exhaustion. She didn't have a nightmare, and if that's what I have to do every night until she gets through this, I gladly will. Anything to help her sleep and move on from what she went through.

Watching her sleep naked in my bed has me as hard as a rock. I've never had this connected to another person or been as protective of anyone in my life. I've never been this addicted to touching and tasting someone.

I slide the covers down the bed and situate my head between her thighs. I spread her wide and go in for a taste. She tastes as sweet and perfect as I remember. I take my time, enjoying teasing her as she starts to wake up.

Her sexy little moans vibrate all the way to my cock, and I want more. I increase the pressure on her clit and thrust two fingers inside her.

"Cole!" she moans as she grabs onto my hair.

"Good morning, firecracker." I smile up at her before continuing my feast.

"Stop teasing me and fuck me properly," she demands, trying to pull me up the bed.

"I like the dirty talk. But you didn't say please." I flip her over onto her stomach, spread her legs wide, and give her a light swat on her perfectly round ass.

Her sweet giggles quickly turn into moans when I thrust into her, fucking her into the mattress. She grips the sheets for dear life and tries to angle her hips as I press her further into the mattress.

"Do you have any idea how damn good you feel? Fuck, I'm not going to last long inside you."

How she does this to me, I will never know. My self-control is gone, and my only thought is to claim her over and over again.

I can't wait to do this every morning. She won't walk around without my seed inside her, without me reminding her she's mine and how much I love her.

Because I realized last night, long after she was asleep, that I love this girl with my whole heart. But instead of telling her, I reach down and stroke her clit. Making her come is my priority, and she doesn't disappoint.

"Cole!" she gasps my name like a prayer and clamps down on my dick. She comes beautifully, and I want to remember every detail.

Jana squeezes me so hard that she pulls the cum from me, and I'm powerless to stop my orgasm. I moan into her neck as my soul leaves my body to twine with hers.

We roll over in a sweaty mess, clinging to each other. Her skin is flushed, and her hair is a mess, but she's never looked more beautiful.

We lie there for a bit, clinging to each other and exchanging soft touches.

I kiss her head. "I'll make breakfast. Come out when you're ready."

She joins me as the food is ready, and we sit down to eat.

"Have you ever done any hunting?" I ask her over breakfast.

"Not really. My parents split when I was little, and they're both in the bigger cities. I moved out here to get away from them."

" I can teach you. It's pretty easy to learn and a useful skill to have out here. What about fishing?"

"Only for fun, but I was never any good at catching anything."

"We fish differently around here, with nets and everything."

Something's off with Jana, and I can't quite put my finger on it. She's not her usual perky self, and she's barely making eye contact with me.

"What's on your mind, firecracker?"

She takes a deep breath and sets her fork down before looking up at me. "I have to go back into town. I have to work, and I can't lose my job because my apartment is attached to it. It's part of my paycheck, room and board. I can't let the community garden go. Too many people use it, and I love helping them every week."

My heart sinks. After last night I thought we'd moved past this. I don't take sex lightly. I've never been one to sleep around. Sex means something. It means commitment, and I thought she understood that.

"Even after last night?" I ask, trying to keep my emotions out of it.

"Especially after last night. I watched my mom give up her career and the person she was before she met my dad. When he left, it nearly killed her. It broke her in ways she still hasn't recovered from. It took my mom a long time to get back on her feet, and I can't put myself in that position and be that vulnerable."

"So that's it then?" I sit back in my chair and cross my arms over my chest.

"It doesn't have to be it."

"You think I can move into town and we'll live happily ever after? I've told you that's not going to happen. This is my home, my life. This is where I feel safe and comfortable."

Jana's eyes mist over, and she turns around to look out the window. "I don't want this to be over, but I don't see any other way at this point. Do you?" Her voice is wobbly.

I don't answer. I hoped to have a few more days to convince her, but nothing I say will change her mind. Without finishing breakfast, I get up and head to the radio to call Cash. I'm not going to force her to stay here if this isn't where she wants to be.

Jana heads back to my room without saying a word. She gets dressed and packs the few things she has here. She emerges as Cash pulls up to the front of the cabin.

"You know where I live, and you're welcome anytime," she says before picking up Muffin and her bag and heading out the door.

She's limping and shouldn't be on her foot yet, but I get the impression if I try to pick her up, she won't let me. Not now.

I stand on the front porch and watch until I can no longer see them or hear the four-wheeler.

Just like that, my world is filled with silence again, as if she was never here and the last few days never happened. But they did, and now everything has changed.

I'm no longer content to be out here alone, but I can't go back into the house where I can still catch her scent in our bed.

Instead, I head to the laundry room, grab a pair of my work jeans and a T-shirt, and head out to the garden. I pull weeds and check on the plants. It's mindless work and perfect since my head is not in the game.

I go over any possible scenario of making things work with her. I'm so lost in my head that I don't even notice someone standing behind me.

"Jesus fucking Christ! Don't sneak up on me like that." I growl at Cash's friend, Axel.

"I wasn't sneaking. You were so far in your head, you didn't hear me."

"What do you want?" I ask, not overly thrilled to have company.

"Hope told my wife what was going on. Those two gossip like old biddies. After my wife heard what happened, she insisted I come to talk to you."

"Why?" I ask, wiping my hands on my jeans.

"Because we have similar reasons for moving out here."

"You got damn lucky your woman wanted to live out here too." I make my way to the porch so I can sit down for this conversation.

"When I walked down the street, people would cross the street so they wouldn't have to walk by me. If they couldn't cross the street, women gripped their purses and practically ran past me. In the grocery store, people avoided the aisle I was in. I dated a few women, but it didn't turn out well. I was too big for them, in more than one way." He shoots me with a knowing look.

"So, you moved out here to the mountains. We all have a sob story of why we're here, but if you think I'm going to tell you mine, you're sadly mistaken."

"You don't make it easy for people to make friends with you, do you?" Axel asks, shaking his head. "Emily literally stumbled into my life. She was lost in the woods, and I was bathing naked in the river. I'd given up hope of finding anyone, and I knew instantly I wouldn't be the same after her. But I also knew that if she'd wanted to walk out the door and leave me, I would have let her. I wouldn't have tried to stop her. And that would've been the biggest mistake of my life."

He leans forward, resting his elbows on his knees, and traces his thumb over his wedding band.

"Emelie was the first girl who made me feel like my size didn't matter. She was proud to walk beside me in public. She didn't care how other people looked at me and walking with her on my arm, I found I didn't either. She loves my size. She loves me. I learned a long time ago no one else matters as long as I have her."

I know that feeling well. It's something I've felt over the last few days.

"That's how Jana makes me feel. Like nothing else matters. But it isn't just the scar. My past isn't pretty, and I can't live in a town as she does. She reminded me today that she has to be there because it's where her job and house are, and she enjoys being around people."

"Axel stands and nods. "I'm not going to pry into your past. That's yours alone, and I learned a long time ago that men moved up here because they don't want to talk about it. There has to be some sort of middle ground. She can't be the one giving up everything."

He turns and leaves without another word.

Chapter 9

Jana

I work at the cafe because I can sit behind the counter and put my foot up. It still hurts, and I shouldn't be walking on it so soon, but I couldn't stay in the cabin any longer.

Leaving yesterday was the hardest thing I've ever had to do. I didn't sleep a wink last night, and the nightmares are back because Cole's not there with me. I've been downing coffee like water, trying to stay awake.

Every time the doorbell chimes with a customer, my heart races, hoping it's him. But I'm disappointed every time. Why would it be him? I gave him no reason to make the effort.

I paste on my fake smile and act like nothing's wrong as people stop in to get their coffee and baked goods. Some customers pop in to check on me once they hear I'm working at the cafe.

By the time I head upstairs to my apartment, my foot is throbbing, my head is pounding, and my heart aches. I collapse on the couch, take a deep breath, and bite the bullet I've been putting off since I got home last night. I call my mom.

"Hey, sweetie. I was starting to worry. I haven't heard from you in a few days," my mom answers the phone.

I can tell she's doing something, probably making herself dinner or cleaning the house. She always multitasks when she's talking on the phone. It's so different from how she was when I was growing up.

"I'm OK. I called to tell you I won't be visiting this weekend. I hurt my ankle, and I need to give it a rest.

I decided today that I was going to spare my mom the details. She doesn't need to get all worked up over my kidnapping. I know I'd never hear the end of it. There's no telling when she'll fall off the deep end again like when my dad left, and I won't be responsible for doing that to her.

"And how did you do that? You have to be more careful."

"I wasn't paying attention, and I sprained it. The swelling has gone down, but I need to ice it. I went back to work today, and even though I had it elevated, it's still hurting."

It's not a complete lie. I wasn't paying attention when I got kidnapped, and I sprained it. I just left out all the details in between. I feel horrible lying to my mother, but in the end, I know this is for the best.

She hums, and all the background noise stops. I hold my breath, waiting to see what she says next. My mom can sometimes be unpredictable when she gets something in her head. "There's something else, isn't there?" she asks.

I decide to divert her attention and tell her about Cole. I tell her he helped me when I sprained my ankle. I tell her that Cash is Hope's neighbor and that's how I know him, that he let me stay with him for a few days while I was healing so I wasn't alone. I tell her about his scar and how he went into town to get Muffin.

"He seems like a nice boy. What's the problem?" Mom asks after I tell her it wouldn't work between us, and I came home.

"He's a mountain man, through and through. He refuses to live in town and never leaves the mountain. I can't give up my whole life for a man only for him to leave like dad. My whole life is here in town."

"I need to confess something. I didn't spiral because I lost your dad. I lost your dad because I spiraled."

"What?"

"Honey, your dad was so great at protecting you, and I was thankful. He took the hit so you wouldn't know the truth. But I didn't realize it was having this kind of effect on your relationships." Her voice is shaky, and she takes a few deep breaths before she continues.

"Honey, I cheated on your father. We were so young when we got married. We changed, and I met a guy. I thought I was in love with him, and he was in love with me. He treated me much better than your father, or so I thought. When he dumped me for the next girl, I spiraled. That's what you remember, but you were so young, I think you got the timing mixed up. I couldn't pull myself out. Eventually, your father said it wasn't healthy for you, and he left, taking you with him."

My mind races. I was about six when all this happened, and I was sure I had the timeline right in my head. I thought my dad left, saw how bad my mom was, and came and took me.

"That's not what I remember."

"I know, sweetheart. Your dad took on so much to protect you. I couldn't get myself out of this depression. I knew I'd screwed things up, not just with your dad but with my marriage and even with you. I started self-medicating, and that's when your dad said it was too much. He packed everything up, picked you up from school that day, and left."

"Why don't I remember any of this?"

"Your dad loved me so much that he treated me better than I deserved. he said he didn't want you to see me that way and would protect you until I got help. He had this misguided belief you needed your mother more than you needed him. I thank him that we have the relationship we do, but you needed him too."

She apologizes over and over again before we get off the phone. I reassure her that I don't blame her for any of this and promise her I'll visit as soon as possible.

After the phone call, I sit and try to remember that time in my life. Nothing I remember corresponds with what my mom told me. Because of my beliefs about how I thought everything happened, my dad and I don't have a good relationship. We talk a few times a year, and as of right now, we haven't spoken in months.

He lives in Bozeman with his new family, and he seems happy. He's always inviting me to different family events and sending me letters and gifts, but I always blew it off.

But I have to know. I have to know my mom wasn't saying something to make me feel better. I have to know if it's true because if so, this changes everything.

I take a deep breath and dial my dad's phone number. It rings a few times before he picks up.

"Jana! We were just talking about how long it's been since we saw you. How are you?"

He sounds so happy and excited to hear from me that tears well in my eyes. I don't have it in me to do the small talk to build up to it. I'm afraid I'll lose the strength to ask the question, so I jump right in.

"Is it true, Dad? That you left because Mom cheated, and then she spiraled?" I can't hide the wobble in my voice, no matter how hard I try.

"She told you?" My dad's voice is soft and serious. I hear murmuring in the background and then a door closing.

"She told me she cheated on you, and the guy dumped her. She went into a huge depression spiral, and you left when she started self-medicating, saying it wasn't good for me to be around her. But that's not what I remember happening."

"I tried so hard to protect you, Jana. Once I found out your mother had cheated, I was willing to forgive and forget because I thought it was better for you to have both of your parents. I loved your mother very much, but she went into this depression spiral, and nothing I said or did helped. It got to a point where being around her set her off and made things worse."

There are telltale sounds of him pouring himself a glass of whiskey. My dad isn't a big drinker, but he'll generally have a glass in hand for tough conversations.

"I had an in-home nurse come to help try to take care of her because she didn't seem to want to be around me. The nurse discovered your mom had been self-medicating with someone else's prescription. Not only that, but she was purposely overdosing herself. I was terrified you would walk in and find her dead on the bed or in the bathroom."

Tears flow freely down my cheeks, imagining the scene and what he had to go through.

"One day, when you are at school, I rented an apartment and furnished it. It took everything I had to come home that day and act like nothing was wrong, not just to your mother but to you. I told you your mother wasn't feeling well and kept you out of her room that night, and the next day while you were at school, I took your mother to a facility her doctor recommended to get her help. Then I picked you up from school and took you to the new apartment."

"I remember that, but I thought you left us before that for some reason."

"I spent some time trying to help your mother, talking with doctors and touring facilities for her. I also had a huge project due at work, so I did some late nights, but no, I hadn't moved out. Your mother kept refusing treatment at the facility. That's when I gave her the ultimatum to stay and get better, or I was going to file for divorce to protect you. She checked herself out of the facility the next day, so I started on the divorce paperwork."

He pauses, and I can picture him sitting on the couch in his office, taking a sip of the whiskey. I wish I'd done this in person and gone to see him because I want nothing more than to hug him right now.

"It took a year for the divorce to go through because of all the psychiatric evaluations. I wanted full custody of you because she was deemed unfit. My lawyer tried to get me to go after child support, but I refused. I wanted her to get better so she could have you back in her life. Once the divorce was final, it was like your mother did a one-eighty. She finally got help, but it was another year before she started to get better. As long as she was getting help, we met at a park, and I let her have some time with you. Eventually, about the time you entered middle school, she was back on her feet, and I helped her file with the court to get partial custody."

"I had no idea. I blamed you for so much. I had it in my head that you left Mom and caused her downward spiral."

"I never wanted you to think badly of your mother. She made some bad decisions, but she wasn't a bad person. As a girl, you needed your mother, so I ensured she stayed in your life as much as possible."

"I needed you too, Dad. I never wanted to let myself depend on a guy in case he walked. I never wanted to fall apart like Mom did."

We sit in silence, unsure what to say next.

"What brought on this conversation with your mother?" Dad asks, finally breaking the silence.

"I met a guy. A great, perfect guy."

I tell Dad everything about Cole and how we met. I don't feel like I have to hold back what happened from my dad. I always knew my dad was stronger than my mother, but I don't think I realized how strong he was until today.

I tell him about the kidnapping, how I injured my foot, how I needed stitches, and how Cole took care of me. I tell him how he doesn't like to be in town, about his scar, his military time, and how he went into town to get my dog.

Dad asks all the questions you would expect a parent to ask, like if I'm OK, were the people who kidnapped me caught, and why they kidnapped me. I answer all his questions truthfully.

He apologizes to me and tells me he did what he thought was best, but if he'd known it would have this type of impact on me, he would've done things differently. He tells me to follow my heart, that so long as I stay true to who I am, there's no wrong decision because being loved by someone is the greatest gift of all.

We stay on the phone for another hour, talking and catching up with everything that's been going on. Dad asks about Hope and Cash and the mountain men's way of life. We talk about the community garden, and I make plans to visit him soon, which seems to excite him most of all.

Before bed, I shoot an e-mail to Hope, telling her I talked to my dad and need to tell her what happened. I tell her there's no rush and to find me the next time she's back in town.

I don't remember falling asleep, but when I wake, I have two texts from my dad. He tells me he's glad we talked last night and I know the truth and reminds me to let him know if I need anything.

I get ready and head down to the cafe to sit behind the counter yet again. My dad and I text on and off all morning. We have so much lost time to make up.

I'm reassuring my stepmother that I'm OK when the bell over the door sounds. I set my phone down and look up to greet whoever walked through the door, but it isn't just anybody.

It's Cole.

Chapter 10

Cole

As I step into the cafe and see Jana sitting behind the counter, everything I rehearsed on the way here flies out the window.

She's finally in front of me after what seems like forever, even though it's only been a few days. All I want to do is rush over and pull her into my arms, but the moment she looks up, and her eyes lock with mine, I'm frozen in place.

"Cole?" She sounds shocked to see me, and it's enough to snap me out of it.

"I can't live in town, but I set aside a piece of land for the community garden. It's five times the size of the space you have now. It's right by the road, so it's easy to access, and I can build a fence to keep visitors from wandering further onto the property, so we can still have our privacy. Next to it is the perfect spot for a greenhouse so you can grow fruits and vegetables all year long."

I take a deep breath and move toward her. She hasn't yelled at me to get out, so I hope that's a good sign.

"I'll bring you into town anytime you need or want. You won't need room and board because you'll be living with me. The garden can be your full-time job. Think of how many people you can help. We'll have our garden by the house you can also take care of. We can expand it, and you can make jams and sell those in Jack's store. We can come down and meet with the guys like Hope and Cash. You can even take stuff to the farmer's market."

I take a few more steps toward her and freeze when she finally stands up.

She comes around the corner, and I instinctively offer her my hand because she's still limping. She ignores it and throws herself into my arms, wrapping herself around me.

"It sounds perfect," she whispers and kisses me right there in the middle of the café in front of the customers.

I wrap my arms around her waist and pick her up, swinging her around in a circle before carefully setting her back on her feet. "Good, because the guys are out back ready to move you out of your apartment."

"Right now?" she asks, her eyes wide.

"Yes."

"But... I have to put in my notice," she says as she looks around the café.

"As long as that notice starts right now so I can take you home where you belong, that's fine."

"Cole! I have to give him two weeks so he can find someone to fill the position."

"Who was filling in for you while you were gone?"

"The assistant manager."

"Sounds like there's already someone to take the position. There's no way I can wait two weeks." I trace my hand's up her waist, skimming the underside of her breasts, hoping it'll drive her crazy like she's driving me crazy.

She pulls out her phone, and her thumb starts flying across the screen as she sends a text. A moment later, a small blonde woman appears in the café.

"Go, Jana. I got this," the girl says, stepping behind the counter and shooing her out the door.

Jana grabs her bag from behind the counter and takes my hand to lead me out the back door. I waste no time swooping in and picking her up.

"You should give your foot a rest," I tell her.

She shakes her head but lets me carry her. "When I get home, I promise to put it up and ice it."

She doesn't realize what it does to me hearing her call my cabin home. I nod and head out the back, where the guys are leaning against their trucks, waiting for me. Their girls are there, too ready to help pack. We have more boxes and tape than we'll ever need, which was all Hope's doing.

I carry her to her apartment and set her down on her couch. "You don't need any of your furniture, but we can take anything you want."

"All this furniture was either hand-me-downs from neighbors, picked off the side of the road, or from the thrift store down the road. I have no attachments to any of it," she says, looking around her small one-bedroom apartment.

"Emelie and I will get started on your clothes in your room," Jenna says.

"I'll get started on the stuff in your kitchen," Hope says.

"All the food can go next door. Whatever Maisie can't eat, she'll take to someone in her church," Jana says.

Just like that, we're packing up her apartment. The two little old ladies from last time stop in to see what all the commotion is. Within an hour, they have someone who wants the furniture, so we don't have to worry about hauling it out. The girls spend an hour cleaning the place up, so it's ready for Jana to turn in her keys.

Then we all head up the mountain. The guys help unload Jana's stuff at my place, and the girls help her start unpacking.

"I remember I couldn't get her stuff unpacked with mine fast enough," Axel says, and the other guys agree.

That's exactly how I'm feeling. The more her stuff is unpacked and mixed with mine, the calmer I become, knowing she's here with me and I can protect and take care of her.

Jana sits on the couch with ice on her ankle the whole time, directing where everything should go, just like she promised.

"How's your ankle?" I ask once everyone has left.

"Pretty good."

"You up for a short walk? I'd like to show you the space I set aside for your garden."

Jana's eyes light up as she stands. I offer her my hand so she can lean on me and take some pressure off her ankle. I lead her to the four-wheeler and take her down the path I cleared yesterday.

"Cash has a lead on another four-wheeler, so you'll have your own and can come down here anytime you want," I tell her as I park the four-wheeler next to the clearing. "The garden won't be up until next season, but we can start working on it now."

I show her my idea for the greenhouse and how I can make it solar-powered.

Jana's eyes light up, so excited about the idea that she's already planning where everything can go and building a little shed.

This piece of land is far enough from the road that we won't be bothered, but we don't want people wandering onto the property either, so Jana agrees about putting up a privacy fence.

Her back is to me as she looks at everything, and I reach into my pocket to pull out the box I shoved there before we left. I drop to one knee and wait for her to turn around.

When she does, she gasps and covers her mouth with her hands.

"I knew the moment I saw you in that cabin and our eyes locked that you were mine. I've never been more certain of anything in my entire life. Now we've worked out the details, I don't want to waste any more time. I want to marry you. I want to live out here and help you build your community garden and raise our kids. Marry me?"

"Yes!" She wastes no time answering.

I slip the ring on her finger before picking her up and placing a kiss on her lips. I can't get her back to the cabin fast enough to make love to my fiancée.

Epilogue

Jana

A few weeks later

"What are you smiling about?" I ask Cole, who has a big grin on his face as he sits in front of his computer.

"I've been talking to your dad, and he's shared a few photos of you from a school play."

I groan. My dad and I have been talking pretty much every day by phone or e-mail. He was thrilled when he heard I took the leap and went all in on the relationship with Cole. As soon as I was feeling better, Dad took us out for dinner so he could meet him. The two of them hit it off and have been talking ever since. Cole was nervous at first, especially having to head into Bozeman, which is a pretty big city and a college town.

But I'd told my dad about Cole's scar and his military time when I talked to him the night before Cole came back to me. He prepared his family, and not one of them flinched. My stepbrother thought it was pretty cool.

Before dinner, Dad had the standard questions every dad asks the guy their daughter brings home, wanting to make sure he's a good guy. Once dinner was done, he welcomed him with open arms, especially when they found out we were engaged. The two of them disappeared into my dad's office and had a long talk. To this day, Cole won't tell me why they both came out with smiles on their faces and have been the best of friends since.

Last weekend, Cole met my mom. Things with us are tense, and I've got a lot to work through. I missed out on so much time with my dad because I accused him of things he never did. Mom is still my mom, but there are a lot of lies I have to come to terms with.

Our relationship has changed for sure, but she also welcomed Cole with open arms and treats him as if he's been part of this family all along.

My parents have agreed to be at my wedding. It'll be the first time they'll be in the same room since the day my dad left and took me with him when I was six. They've both assured me they can be in a room together and everything will be fine, and they've spent time together successfully.

Cole may get along with both of them, but he made it clear he won't stand for anyone ruining our big day. I think he earned more of my dad's respect that day because my dad is very protective of me. Knowing Cole is just as protective made him very happy.

My dad is also overseeing the kidnapping case and ensuring Hope's mom and her boyfriend pay the price. The last I heard, they had more charges against them in Georgia, and the kidnapping charge is the icing on the cake that will ensure they're locked away for the rest of their lives. Hope has agreed to testify against her mother. They never had the best relationship, and her mother always chose drugs and guys over her, so there's no love lost between them.

Cole and I started preparing the garden for next season, plowing the land, and fertilizing the soil. We also got the material we need to build the fence before winter. The guys are planning a building party to help build the greenhouse while the women do the winter prep.

They think they can have the greenhouse up and running in a weekend, and I'm excited about it. We've already been working on expanding our personal garden so I can work on canning fruits and vegetables and jams because I love the idea of doing that and selling it in the shop. The guys are also happy to have Cole coming to the shop every month.

Today, we're taking the first batch of canned goods to the store. We're also meeting with the guys and ordering everything we need for the greenhouse from Jack.

I can tell on the drive that Cole is nervous, so I lean over and give him a kiss on the cheek while he's driving. "You know the guys. And I promise I will not leave your side. Everything will be fine."

"I know. It's just going to take some getting used to. Bear with me," he says with a strained smile.

"I have nowhere else I would rather be than right here with you. I know this takes time, but I want you to know how much it means to me that you're trying."

That seems to help him relax, and he holds my hand the rest of the way down the mountain. As soon as we pull into the parking lot and get ready to head inside, he tenses right up again.

We go in the back door that Hope told us to use. She spots us as soon as we come through the door and comes over to give me a hug and say hi to Cole.

"Jack, this is my neighbor, Cole. Cole, this is the guy who owns the store. Jack is a good friend and can order anything you need," Cash says.

"Good to meet you, Cole," Jack says without missing a beat. "What have you got here for me?"

"We've been doing some canning and jams, and I'm wondering what will sell. It's all locally grown," I tell him.

Jack's store is part outdoor store and part locally crafted items. Axel sells his homemade jerky and hand-carved knives. Phoenix makes handmade home decor and wooden furniture. Cash sells a lot of items made from the furs of the animals he catches—blankets and coats seem to be the biggest sellers. And Bennett sells handmade weapons such as arrows, knives, and the like.

Axel's wife, Emelie, has started making home decor from locally recycled items. Jenna, Phoenix's wife, sells her local photography, and Hope has started selling some baked goods.

None of these guys need the money, but it's always good to have some for a rainy day. They use it as an excuse to get together once a month, so long as they're not snowed in.

"We're still on to go wedding dress shopping in a few days, right?" Hope asks me after we get everything settled and the guys are talking.

Hope found this cute little boutique with clothes on the rack so we can try them on, and Maisie and Mrs. Tipton agreed to do our alterations should we need any. We're getting married two weeks apart up on the mountain. Other than my parents, there's no one outside the guys and the people here in the store right now I want at our wedding. Hope and Cash don't have any other family joining them, so the only thing holding us up is our dresses.

Hope and I want to get married up on the mountain, so we're having the wedding near our cabins. We have the same taste, so we'll split the cost on decorations.

We're lost in wedding plan talk when one of the guys clears their throat, drawing our attention.

"I want to announce that my wife will be here in just a few weeks," Bennett says, and everyone goes silent.

"Your *wife?* We had no idea you were seeing someone," Emelie says, looking shocked.

"It's been a bit of a long-distance thing." Bennett shrugs uncomfortably.

There's more to this story, and if anyone can get to the bottom of it, it's Emelie.

"As soon as you are both settled, I demand you bring her over for dinner." Emelie glares at Bennett, who just smiles.

"I promise."

Everyone asks questions, and Bennett says he promises to share the entire story once his mystery woman is here.

Later that night, we're sitting on the porch where we sat the morning we watched the sunrise after my nightmare. I'm snuggled up on Cole's lap, and he's wrapped us in a blanket as we watch the light leave the sky.

"Thank you for bringing me back to life," he says out of the blue.

I turn to face him. "Thank you for giving me this life. I'm so much happier here than I ever was working at the store and the café."

"I might never be ready for a big city outside of visiting your parents, but every time I go into Whiskey River, it gets easier. This is our home, and I promise to be more present and active in it."

He couldn't have given me a better gift if he tried.

. . . ● . ● . . . .

Want a bonus Epilogue of Jana and Cole? **Sign up for my newsletter to get it for free!**

Want Cash and Hope's story? Grab it in **Take Me To The Lake.**

Or start the whole series from the start with Axle and Emelie in **Take Me To The River!**

Grab Bennett's story in **Take Me To The Mountain.**

Other Books by Kaci Rose

See all of Kaci Rose's Books

Oakside Military Heroes Series
Saving Noah – Lexi and Noah
Saving Easton – Easton and Paisley
Saving Teddy – Teddy and Mia
Saving Levi – Levi and Mandy
Saving Gavin – Gavin and Lauren
Saving Logan – Logan and Faith

Mountain Men of Whiskey River
Take Me To The River – Axel and Emelie
Take Me To The Cabin – Pheonix and Jenna
Take Me To The Lake – Cash and Hope

Taken by The Mountain Man - Cole and Jana
Take Me To The Mountain – Bennett and Willow

Chasing the Sun Duet
Sunrise – Kade and Lin
Sunset – Jasper and Brynn

Rock Stars of Nashville
She's Still The One – Dallas and Austin

Club Red – Short Stories
Daddy's Dare – Knox and Summer
Sold to my Ex's Dad - Evan and Jana
Jingling His Bells

Club Red: Chicago
Elusive Dom

Standalone Books
Texting Titan - Denver and Avery
Accidental Sugar Daddy – Owen and Ellie
Saving Mason - Mason and Paige

Stay With Me Now – David and Ivy
Midnight Rose - Ruby and Orlando
Committed Cowboy – Whiskey Run Cowboys
Stalking His Obsession - Dakota and Grant
Falling in Love on Route 66 - Weston and Rory
Billionaire's Marigold
Saving Ethan

Connect with Kaci Rose

Website

Facebook

Kaci Rose Reader's Facebook Group

TikTok

Instagram

Twitter

Goodreads

Book Bub

Join Kaci Rose's VIP List (Newsletter)

About Kaci Rose

Kaci Rose writes steamy contemporary romance mostly set in small towns. She grew up in Florida but longs for the mountains over the beach.
She is a mom to 5 kids and a dog who is scared of his own shadow.

She also writes steamy cowboy romance as Kaci M. Rose.

Please Leave a Review!

I love to hear from my readers! Please **head over to your favorite store and leave a review** of what you thought of this book!

Made in United States
Orlando, FL
13 March 2023

31013924R00065